HORROR STORIES

Choix des textes et notes par

Sylvie Persec

Agrégée d'anglais

Avec la collaboration de Louise Trehorel.

Mise en pages : Tiffany Thomas
Couverture : Bérengère Verret
Photo de couverture : Fotolia

1 rue du bac, 75007 Paris
www.ophrys.fr

ISBN : 978-2-7080-1470-1

La collection s'adresse à tous ceux qui ont envie de lire des textes littéraires en version originale. Les ouvrages regroupent par thèmes les textes d'auteurs connus et reconnus dans chacune des langues proposées.

Les textes sont présentés en version intégrale ou en version adaptée et simplifiée, selon le niveau de difficulté. L'essentiel du vocabulaire nécessaire est traduit sur la page de gauche pour une lecture facile et rapide.

Quatre niveaux pour quatre groupes de lecteurs :
Niveau 1 : super facile pour débutants et adolescents (A2 vers B1)
Niveau 2 : facile (B1)
Niveau 3 : intermédiaire (B1 vers B2)
Niveau 4 : avancé (B2 vers C1)

Collection dirigée par Sylvie Persec.

INTRODUCTION

Horror! Le mot surgit dans chacune de ces nouvelles de la bouche de l'un des personnages : passager d'une traversée transatlantique – tant la mer a suscité dans la littérature de langue anglaise de récits d'épouvante – promeneur tranquille et discret au bord des berges familières d'un lac ou en villégiature dans cette paisible campagne anglaise qui secrète un ennui… mortel.

Ils sont tous dans des vies banales, dilettantes blasés de l'aristocratie anglaise dans les nouvelles de Saki, parfois accompagnés d'hommes de science témoins de leur histoire et garants de la rationalité ordinaire, marins des sombres nuits de l'Atlantique chez F. Marion Crawford, époux ou hôte anonyme chez Edgar A. Poe.

Et ils font tous l'expérience d'un point d'arrêt, dont ils font parfois eux-mêmes le récit, d'un point d'horreur. Jaillissent alors, comme des apparitions, des morceaux de corps humain : crâne, squelette, dents, bras, œil – qui d'inertes deviennent remuants et hurlants ou suintant de moiteur maritime – animaux menaçants, chat noir, chien, loup… Le vivant et le mort, l'enfant et la bête sauvage… L'étrangeté des décors familiers. Le surnaturel affleure et le fantastique fait partie du voyage.

Les auteurs sont des maîtres du genre. Chacun a ses thèmatiques propres et ses obsessions. Chacun a son style, qui n'exclut pas l'humour… noir. Les chutes de ces histoires sont parfois hallucinantes.

TABLE DES MATIÈRES

EDGAR ALLAN POE (1809-1849) was an American writer, poet, critic and editor. He is one of America's best-known writers. He is famous for his tales and poems of horror and mystery. His works are as fascinating today as they were more than 150 years ago. He is indisputably the founding father of crime fiction, perhaps the most successful narrative genre in the modern world.

Les 20 mots clés de l'histoire

a murderer = un meutrier

mad = fou

to be hanged = être pendu

the hangman = le bourreau

to haunt = hanter

revenge = la vengeance

hatred = la haine

anger = la colère

fear / fright = la peur

guilt = la culpabilité

hideous = hideux

ghastly = affreux

Evil = le Mal

to do wrong = faire le mal

a sin = un péché

an axe = une hache

the cellar = la cave

a tomb = une tombe

to conceal = dissimuler

the Gallows = la potence, le gibet

THE BLACK CAT

Le chat noir

"The fury of a demon instantly possessed me."
This story is the confession of a murderer who knows that he will be hanged the next day.

As he tells the story of his life, he goes from extreme fury to horror and then from remorse to satisfaction and triumph.

The figure of his beloved black cat is haunting him.
Will his victims get their revenge?

~

- **to be about to** = être sur le point de
- **I do not expect belief** = je n'attends pas que l'on me croie
- **to unburden my soul** = soulager mon âme

- **a purpose** = un but

- **to be fond of** = adorer

- **to feed (fed, fed)** = nourrir

- **gold-fish** = des poissons rouges
- **rabbits** = des lapins
- **a monkey** = un singe

- **clever** = intelligent

- **to regard as** = considérer
- **witches in disguise** = des sorcières déguisées

- **a playmate** = un compagnon de jeu
- **alone** = moi seul

- **to last** = durer
- **to grow** = devenir
- **at length** = avec le temps
- **to ill-use** = maltraiter
- **to restrain from** = se retenir de

For the narrative I am about to write, I do not expect belief. I am not mad—and very surely I do not dream. But to-morrow I will die, and to-day I want to unburden my soul.

My immediate purpose is to tell the world about a series of events which have terrified—and destroyed me. To me, they have only presented Horror.

In my infancy, I was especially fond of animals, and I had a great variety of pets. I spent most of my time feeding and caressing them.

I married early, and was happy to find that my wife was fond of animals too. We had birds, gold-fish, a fine dog, rabbits, a small monkey, and a cat.

This cat was a remarkably large and beautiful animal, entirely black, and extremely clever. In speaking of his intelligence, my wife, who was superstitious, made frequent allusion to the ancient popular notion, which regarded all black cats as witches in disguise.

Pluto—this was the cat's name—was my favorite pet and playmate. I alone fed him, and he followed me wherever I went about the house and through the streets.

Our friendship lasted, in this manner, for several years, but gradually I grew more irritable. At length, I even offered my wife personal violence. My pets, of course, felt the change. I not only neglected, but ill-used them. I restrained from maltreating Pluto, but I maltreated the rabbits, the monkey, or even the dog, when by accident, or through affection, they came in my way.

- **disease** = maladie

- **to experience** = ressentir
- **ill temper** = mauvaise humeur
- **intoxicated** = soûl
- **to fancy** = imaginer
- **to avoid** = éviter
- **he slightly bit** = il mordit légèrement

- **to grasp** = attraper
- **the throat** = le cou
- **cut one of its eyes from** = lui arrachai un de ses yeux
- **the socket** = l'orbite
- **to blush** = rougir
- **to shudder** = frissonner
- **damnable** = maudite
- **to drown** = noyer
- **the deed** = le crime

- **to recover** = se remettre

- **pain** = la douleur
- **as might be expected** = comme on pouvait s'y attendre
- **to flee (fled, fled)** = s'enfuir
- **grieved** = chagriné

- **to urge** = pousser à
- **in cool blood** = de sang froid
- **to hang (hung, hung)** = pendre
- **a rope** = une corde
- **to stream** = couler

But my disease grew worse—what disease? Alcohol!—and even Pluto, who was now becoming old—even Pluto began to experience the effects of my ill temper.

One night, returning home, much intoxicated, I fancied that the cat avoided my presence. I seized him; in his fright, he slightly bit me on the hand.

The fury of a demon instantly possessed me. I took a pen-knife from my pocket, grasped the poor beast by the throat, and deliberately cut one of its eyes from the socket! I blush, I burn, I shudder, while I write the damnable atrocity.

When reason returned with the morning, I experienced a sentiment half of horror, half of remorse; but it was, a feeble and equivocal feeling, and I soon drowned in wine all memory of the deed.

The cat slowly recovered. The socket of the lost eye looked terrible, but he no longer appeared to suffer any pain. He went about the house as usual, but, as might be expected, fled in extreme terror at my approach.

At first I was grieved. But this feeling soon gave place to irritation. And then came the spirit of Perverseness.

It was this desire to do wrong that urged me to continue. One morning, in cool blood, I found a rope and calmly put it round Pluto's neck and hung the cat to a tree; —hung it with the tears streaming from my eyes, and with remorse at my heart. I hung it *because* I knew that it had loved me, and because it had never offended

- **to commit a sin** = commettre un péché
- **deadly** = mortel

- **aroused from sleep** = tiré du sommeil

- **made our escape** = nous échappâmes

- **against which** = contre laquelle

- **the plastering / plaster** = le / du plâtre
- **to spread (spread, spread)** = étaler / poser

- **a figure** = une silhouette

- **wonder** = stupéfaction

- **filled by** = rempli de
- **a crowd** = une foule

- **must have been cut from** = avait dû être détaché
- **to throw (threw, thrown)** = jeter

me; —hung it *because* I knew that I was committing a sin—a deadly sin.

On that very same night, I was aroused from sleep by the cry of "Fire!" The whole house was in flames. It was with great difficulty that my wife, a servant, and myself, made our escape. The destruction was complete.

The next day, I visited the ruins. I saw several persons who seemed to be examining a wall. It was the only wall that was still standing. It was one of my chamber walls, the one against which the head of my bed had been.

I heard the words "strange!", "singular!" and other similar expressions. All the other walls had all fallen. The plastering here had resisted the fire—probably because it had been recently spread.

I approached and saw, upon the white surface of the wall, the figure of a gigantic *cat*. There was a rope about the animal's neck.

When I first saw this apparition, my wonder and my terror were extreme.

Then, reflection came to my aid: the cat, I remembered, had been hung in a garden adjacent to the house. I was asleep when the alarm of fire was given and my window was open. The garden had been immediately filled by a crowd of people.

The animal must have been cut from the tree by a neighbour and thrown into my chamber in order to

- **in order to wake me up** = dans le but de me réveiller
- **to hit (hit, hit)** = heurter

- **rid myself** = me débarasser

- **the loss** = la perte

- **the breast** = la poitrine

- **to purr** = ronronner
- **to rub** = se frotter
- **delighted** = ravi

- **to reach** = atteindre

- **to annoy** = contrarier

- **to add** = ajouter
- **to deprive** = priver
- **to refrain from** = se retenir de
- **former** = précédent
- **chiefly** = principalement
- **dread** = terreur
- **uncomplaining** = qui ne se plaignait jamais
- **usual** = habituel
- **sufferer** = souffre-douleur

wake me up. It had probably hit the wall above my bed. The falling of other walls had compressed the cat into the fresh plaster.

But for months I could not rid myself of the phantasm of the cat; and, during this period, I experienced a half-sentiment of remorse. I even regretted the loss of the animal and started to look for another cat of similar appearance.

One night I saw a black cat—a very large one—as large as Pluto, and closely resembling him. Except for one thing. This cat had a large mark of white on his breast.

When I touched him, he purred loudly, rubbed against my hand, and appeared delighted.

I continued my caresses and the animal accompanied me on my way home. When it reached the house it domesticated itself at once, and became immediately a great favorite with my wife.

For my own part, I soon began to dislike it. Its love disgusted and annoyed me.

What added to my hatred, was the discovery, that, like Pluto, it also had been deprived of one of its eyes.
I wanted to destroy it, I refrained from doing so, partly by a memory of my former crime, but chiefly—let me confess it at once—by absolute dread of the beast.

My mind was invaded by Evil thoughts. My uncomplaining wife, alas! was the most usual and the most patient of sufferers. One day she accompanied me

- **the cellar** = la cave
- **steep** = raide
- **nearly throwing me headlong** = me faisant presque tomber la tête la première
- **uplifting an axe** = brandissant une hache
- **to aim at** = viser
- **to withdraw (withdrew, withdrawn)** = dégager
- **buried** = enfonçai
- **the brain** = (le cerveau) le crâne
- **a groan** = un gémissement

- **minute** = minuscules

- **to wall sth up** = emmurer

- **lately** = récemment
- **in one of the walls was a projection** = l'un des murs formait à un endroit une saillie
- **the corpse** = le cadavre
- **the space behind** = la cavité qui se trouvait derrière
- **suspicious** =suspect

- **wretchedness** = malheur
- **previous** = précédente

into the cellar.The cat followed me down the steep stairs, and, nearly throwing me headlong, exasperated me.

Uplifting an axe, I aimed at the animal. But my arm was arrested by the hand of my wife.

My rage became demoniacal. I withdrew my arm and buried the axe in her brain. She fell dead, without a groan.

This hideous murder accomplished, I decided to make plans to conceal the body.

I knew that I could not remove it from the house without the risk of being observed by the neighbors. Many projects entered my mind. At one period I thought of cutting the corpse into minute fragments, and destroying them by fire. Finally I determined to wall it up in the cellar.

The cellar was well adapted. Its walls had lately been plastered. Moreover, in one of the walls was a projection. No doubt I could easily displace the bricks at this point, insert the corpse in the space behind, and then replace the bricks as before, so that no eye could detect anything suspicious.

I carefully deposited the body inside. I put back the bricks and covered the wall with new plaster. When I had finished, I felt satisfied that all was right. I looked around triumphantly.

Then I started to look for the beast which had caused my wretchedness; but the animal had been alarmed at

- **to breathe** = respirer

- **little disturbed me** = ne m'encombrait guère

- **very unexpectedly** = de façon inopinée
- **to search** = fouiller
- **to beat (beat, beaten)** = battre

- **glee** = la joie
- **to be restrained** = pour être contenue

- **through mere bravado** = par pure bravade
- **rapped** = frappai
- **that very portion** = l'endroit même
- **from within** = venue du fond de
- **muffled** = sourd
- **to turn into** = se transformer
- **the sobbing** = les pleurs
- **a shriek** = un hurlement
- **motionless** = immobile
- **to pull out** =retirer
- **already greatly decayed** = dans un état de putréfaction déjà avancé

the violence of my previous anger.

It did not appear during the night—and for one night at least, I slept tranquilly.

The second and the third day passed, and still my tormentor came not. Once again I breathed as a freeman. The monster, in terror, had fled forever! My happiness was supreme! The guilt of my dark deed little disturbed me.

Upon the fourth day of the assassination, the police came, very unexpectedly, into the house, and started to search it. I felt no embarrassment whatever. The officers descended into the cellar. My heart beat calmly. I walked the cellar from end to end. The police were perfectly satisfied and prepared to depart. The glee at my heart was too strong to be restrained.

"By the way, gentlemen," I said at last, "this—this is a very well constructed house. I may say an excellently well constructed house. These walls—are you going, gentlemen?—These walls are solidly put together." And here, through mere bravado, I rapped heavily, with a cane which I held in my hand, upon that very portion of the wall behind which stood the corpse of my wife.

I was answered by a voice from within the tomb!—by a cry, at first muffled, like the sobbing of a child, which turned into a shriek, half of horror and half of triumph.

For one instant the police remained motionless.Then, they ran to the wall and started pulling out the bricks. The wall fell. The corpse, already greatly decayed

- **stood erect** = se dressait

- **within** = à l'intérieur

stood erect before the eyes of the spectators. Upon its head, with a red, open mouth and a solitary eye, sat the hideous cat. Its voice which had led me to murder was now sending me to the hangman.

I had walled the monster up within the tomb!

~

Les 10 mots clés de l'histoire

tell-tale = qui en dit long = révélateur

mad / insane = fou

Evil = le Mal

the vulture eye = l'œil de vautour

a corpse = un cadavre

to dismember = démembrer

to conceal = dissimuler

to shriek / to yell = hurler / crier

carefully = avec soin / précaution

the beating of the heart = le battement du cœur

The Tell-Tale Heart

Le cœur révélateur

Why did he kill the old man?
"I think it was his eye!"
"How, then, am I mad?"

The story is told by an unnamed narrator who describes how carefully he planned a crime.
He insists that he is not insane but he is giving all the details about how he dismembered the body.
Will the beating of the victim's heart eventually tell the truth?

This is one of Edgar Allan Poe's most famous horror stories. It is about madness and horror. It is purely and simply terrifying.

~

- **The disease had sharpened my senses.** = La maladie avait aiguisé mes sens.
- **heaven** = le paradis
- **hell** = l'enfer

- **the brain** = le cerveau
- **to haunt** = hanter
- **He had never done me any wrong.** = Il ne m'avait jamais fait aucun mal.

- **a vulture** = un vautour
- **with a film over it** = recouvert d'un voile
- **whenever** = chaque fois que
- **my blood ran cold** = mon sang se glaçait
- **to get rid of** = se débarrasser de
- **Now this is the point.** = Voilà toute la question.

- **about midnight** = vers minuit
- **gently** = doucement
- **how cleverly** = avec quelle adresse

- **lying (lie, lay, lain)** = (être) couché
- **to disturb** = déranger
- **carefully** = avec précaution
- **a single ray** = un seul rayon de lumière

"TRUE!—nervous—very, very nervous I had been and am; but why *will* you say that I am mad? The disease had sharpened my senses, and above all the sense of hearing. I heard all things in the heaven and in the earth. I heard many things in hell. How, then, am I mad? Listen! and see how calmly I can tell you the whole story.

It is impossible to say how first the idea entered my brain; but it haunted me day and night. I loved the old man. He had never done me any wrong. He had never insulted me. For his gold I had no desire.

I think it was his eye! Yes, it was this! He had the eye of a vulture—a pale blue eye, with a film over it. Whenever he looked at me, my blood ran cold; and so very gradually I decided to kill the old man, and in this way get rid of the eye forever.

Now this is the point. You think I'm mad. But you should have seen me. You should have seen with what dissimulation I planned it!

I was very kind to the old man during the whole week before I killed him. And every night, about midnight, I opened his door—oh so gently! Oh, you would have laughed to see how cleverly I did it. And then, I moved slowly—very, very slowly, so that I could see the old man lying upon his bed. I did not want to disturb the old man's sleep. And then, I opened my lantern carefully—oh, so carefully so that a single ray fell upon the vulture eye.

And this I did for seven long nights—every night just

- **for** = car
- **to anger** = mettre en colère
- **Evil** = le Mal

- **cheerfully** = joyeusement

- **more than usually cautious** = plus prudent que d'habitude
- **the extent** = l'étendue

- **sprang up (spring, sprang, sprung)** = se redressa d'un bond
- **still** = immobile
- **in the meantime** = entre-temps

- **a slight groan** = un faible gémissement
- **pain** = de la douleur
- **grief** = du chagrin
- **awe** = de l'effroi
- **to pity** = avoir pitié
- **although** = même si
- **his fears had been growing upon him** = ses peurs l'avaient envahi
- **to worry** = s'inquiéter

at midnight—but I found the eye always closed; and so it was impossible to do the work; for it was not the old man who angered me, but his Evil Eye.

And every morning, I went into his bedroom and spoke to him cheerfully, asking how he had passed the night. So you see he could not have suspected anything.

Upon the eighth night I was more than usually cautious in opening the door. Before that night I had never felt the extent of my own powers – of my intelligence. I laughed a little at the idea; and perhaps he heard me; for he moved on the bed suddenly, as if surprised. He sprang up in bed, crying out: "Who's there?" I kept quite still and said nothing.

For a whole hour I did not move, and in the meantime I did not hear him lie down. He was still sitting up in the bed listening.

Then I heard a slight groan, and I knew it was the groan of mortal terror. It was not pain or grief—oh, no!—it was awe. I knew the sound well. Very often, just at midnight, when all the world slept, I heard it—the sound of terror. I say I knew it well. I knew what the old man felt, and pitied him, although I laughed inside. I knew that his fears had been growing upon him. He had been trying to think there was no reason to worry, all in vain. All in vain; because Death had enveloped the victim and he felt my presence within the room.

When I had waited a long time, very patiently, I decided to open the lantern a little and a ray of light fell exactly upon the vulture eye. It was open—wide, wide

- **wide open** = grand ouvert

- **the beating** = le battement
- **to increase** = accroître
- **I kept still** = je restai immobile
- **scarcely** = à peine
- **to breathe** = respirer
- **held (hold, held, held)** = tenais
- **motionless** = immobile
- **loud** = fort
- **at the dead hour of the night** = en plein cœur de la nuit
- **dreadful** = redoutable
- **yet** = cependant
- **to burst** = éclater
- **a neighbor** = un voisin

- **a yell** = un hurlement
- **to leap** = bondir
- **to shriek** = crier
- **I dragged him to the floor** = je le jetai au sol
- **to pull** = tirer
- **gaily** = gaiement
- **the heart went on beating** = le cœur continua à battre
- **at length** = finalement
- **to cease** = s'arrêter
- **to remove** = retirer
- **the corpse** = le cadavre
- **stone dead** = raide mort
- **His eye would trouble me no more.** = Son oeil ne me tourmenterait plus.
- **to conceal** = dissimuler
- **to dismember** = démembrer

open—and I grew furious. It was hideous; but I could see nothing else of the old man's face. Then I heard a low, quick sound. I knew that sound well, too. It was the beating of the old man's heart. It increased my fury.

But I kept still. I scarcely breathed. I held the lantern motionless. I maintained the ray upon the eye.

Meantime the sound increased. It grew quicker and quicker, and louder and louder every instant. The old man's terror *must* have been extreme! It grew louder, I say, louder every moment! And now at the dead hour of the night, in the dreadful silence of that old house, this noise terrified me. Yet, for some minutes longer I stood still. But the beating grew louder, louder! I thought the heart must burst. And I thought the sound would be heard by a neighbor! The old man's hour had come!

With a loud yell, I leaped into the room. He shrieked once—once only. In an instant I dragged him to the floor, and pulled the heavy bed over him. I then smiled gaily.

But, for many minutes, the heart went on beating. At length it ceased. The old man was dead. I removed the bed and examined the corpse. Yes, he was stone, stone dead. His eye would trouble me no more.

If still you think me mad, you will think so no longer when I describe the precautions I took to conceal the body. I worked fast but in silence. First of all I dismembered the corpse. I cut off the head and the arms and the legs.

- **to take up (took, taken)** = enlever
- **a plank** = une planche
- **a board** = une latte du plancher
- **cleverly** = adroitement
- **a stain** = une tache
- **blood** = du sang
- **There came a knocking.** = À ce moment-là quelqu'un frappa.
- **to introduce oneself** = se présenter
- **to send (sent, sent)** = envoyer
- **to search** = fouiller

- **to fear** = craindre
- **The shriek [...] was my own** = C'est moi qui avait crié

- **all over the house** = dans toute la maison
- **to lead (led, led)** = guider
- **to rest** = se reposer
- **underneath** = en-dessous

- **manner** = attitude
- **to convince** = convaincre
- **I wished them gone** = J'aurais voulu qu'ils s'en aillent
- **to ache** = faire mal
- **I fancied a ringing in my ears** = j'eus l'impression que quelque chose tintait dans mes oreilles
- **within** = à l'intérieur de
- **more fluently** = avec une aisance accrue
- **steadily** = régulièrement

- **almighty** = tout puissant
- **they were making a mockery of my horror** = ils se raillaient de ma terreur

I took up three planks from the floor, deposited all, and then replaced the boards so cleverly that no human eye—not even *his*—could have detected any thing wrong. There was no stain—no blood. It was four o'clock—still dark as midnight.

There came a knocking at the street door. I went down to open it. There entered three men, who introduced themselves as officers of the police. A shriek had been heard by a neighbor during the night; and they (the officers) had been sent to search the house.

I smiled—for what had I to fear? The shriek, I said, was my own in a dream. The old man was absent in the country.

I took my visitors all over the house. I told them to search—search well. I led them to his chamber. I brought chairs into the room, and asked them to rest. I placed my own chair on the spot underneath which reposed the corpse of the victim. The officers were satisfied. My manner had convinced them.

But, before long, I felt myself getting pale and wished them gone. My head ached, and I fancied a ringing in my ears: but still they sat and chatted. At length, I found that the noise was not within my ears.

I talked more fluently, and with a louder voice. But the noise steadily increased. Oh God! What could I do?

Was it possible they heard not? Almighty God!—no, no! They heard!—they suspected!—they knew!—they were making a mockery of my horror!—this I thought,

- **agony** = torture

- **Villains!** = Misérables !
- **dissemble no more!** = ne faites plus semblant !
- **to admit** = avouer
- **the deed** = le crime
- **to tear up (tore, torn)** = arracher

and this I think. But anything was better than this agony! Anything was more tolerable than this derision!

"Villains!" I shrieked, "dissemble no more! I admit the deed!—tear up the planks!—here, here!—it is the beating of his hideous heart!"

~

FRANCIS MARION CRAWFORD

(1854-1909) was an American prolific author and historian. He published a number of successful novels. His books of fiction were widely popular. Several of his stories are considered to be classics of the horror genre.

Les 15 mots clés de l'histoire

to scream = crier

to shriek = hurler

the skull = le crâne

a ghost = un fantôme

to haunt = hanter

a cupboard = un placard

a jaw = une mâchoire

two lower front teeth = deux incisives du bas

to bite (bit, bitten) = mordre

to lock = fermer à clé

boiling lead = du plomb brûlant

to pour = verser

the throat = la gorge

gloomy = sinistre

ghastly = épouvantable

The Screaming Skull

Le crâne hurlant

"There! Lord, what a shriek!"
"Ghosts? No! But it's something that hears and understands;"

A series of deaths. A skull kept inside a cupboard. A jaw found on the beach. Screams. The narrator—a retired sailor living by the sea, alone—is haunted by them.

"What is there to prove that Luke killed his wife?" he wonders.

A terrifying narrative of doubt, terror, and shrieks.

~

- **to believe** = croire
- **unless** = à moins que
- **whatever it is** = quelle que soit cette chose
- **as much as** = autant que
- **to blame oneself for** = se reprocher

- **she might be alive yet** = elle serait peut-être encore en vie
- **I fancy** = J'imagine
- **with a sweet temper** = qui avait bon caractère
- **gentle** = doux
- **once** = une fois
- **same** = identique
- **unmistakable** = qui ne ressemble à aucun autre

- **were not on good terms** = ne s'entendaient pas bien
- **wet** = humide
- **to moan** = gémir
- **Hush!** = Chut !
- **the tide** = la marée

- **to be out of temper / in a nasty temper** = être de (très) mauvaise humeur
- **which didn't improve matters** = ce qui n'arrangeait rien
- **worse** = pire
- **at all events** = en tout cas

- **to succeed** = réussir
- **hurt** = blessée
- **much too clever** = bien trop intelligente
- **to get rid of** = se débarrasser de
- **who did for three husbands** = qui se débarrassa de trois maris
- **foul play** = homicide

I have often heard it scream. No, I am not nervous, I am not imaginative, and I never believed in ghosts, unless that thing is one. Whatever it is, it hates me almost as much as it hated Luke Pratt, and it screams at me.

I have always blamed myself for Mrs. Pratt's death, and I suppose I was responsible for it in a way. If I had not told that story she might be alive yet. That is why the thing screams at me, I fancy. She was a good little woman, with a sweet temper and a nice gentle voice; but I remember hearing her shriek once. It was the same scream; exactly the same; do you know what I mean? Unmistakable.

The truth is, I had not realized that the doctor and his wife were not on good terms. I was dining with the Pratts one night, when I told them the story. It was a wet night in November, and the sea was moaning. Hush!—if you don't speak you will hear it now... Do you hear the tide? Gloomy sound, isn't it?

The weather was dirty, Pratt was out of temper, and the dinner was bad, very bad indeed, which didn't improve matters, and cold, which made it worse. The poor little lady was very unhappy about it. Pratt must have had a hard day. Perhaps he had lost a patient. At all events, he was in a nasty temper. "My wife is trying to poison me, you see!" he said. "She'll succeed some day." I saw that she was hurt and said that Mrs. Pratt was much too clever to get rid of her husband in such a simple way.

And I told a story about a woman in Ireland who did for three husbands before anyone suspected foul play.

- **to manage** = réussir
- **to keep awake** = rester éveillé
- **to catch (caught, caught)** = attraper
- **to hang (hung, hung/hanged)** = pendre
- **to drug** = droguer
- **to pour** = verser
- **melted lead** = du plomb fondu
- **asleep** = endormi
- **to whistle** = siffler
- **to be lonely** = se sentir seul
- **now and then** = de temps en temps
- **to look worn** = avoir l'air épuisé
- **years went o**n = les années ont passé
- **queer** = bizarre
- **to be fond of** = adorer
- **that used to follow her everywhere** = qui la suivait partout

- **a ship** = un bateau
- **in dock** = à quai
- **three weeks off** = trois semaines de congé
- **to be about** = être dans les parages
- **casually** = d'un air détaché
- **odd** = bizarre
- **I could stand it no longer.** = Je ne pouvais plus le supporter.

- **to glare** = regarder méchamment
- **to howl** = hurler
- **to shiver** = frisonner
- **quiet** = calme

Did you never hear that tale? The fourth husband managed to keep awake and caught her, and she was hanged. How did she do it? She drugged them, and poured melted lead into their ears when they were asleep… No—that's the wind whistling. Yes, it was in November. Poor Mrs. Pratt died suddenly in her bed not long after I dined here.

Luke must have been lonely here after she was dead, I should think; I came to see him now and then, and he looked worn and nervous. Years went on, and his son was killed in South Africa, and after that he began to be queer.

He had an old dog, Bumble, that poor Mrs. Pratt had been fond of, and that used to follow her everywhere. It was the sweetest beast you ever saw.

I came down one day before Christmas, when my ship was in dock and I had three weeks off. Bumble was not about, and I said casually that I supposed the old dog was dead. "Yes," Pratt answered, and I thought there was something odd in his tone even before he went on after a little pause. "I killed him," he said presently. "I could stand it no longer." I asked what it was that Luke could not stand. "He had a way of sitting in her chair and glaring at me, and then howling." Luke shivered a little. "He didn't suffer at all, poor old Bumble. I chloroformed him. It's been quieter since then."

What is there to prove that Luke killed his wife? I would not even suggest such a thing to anyone but you. After all, there was nothing but the coincidence that poor little Mrs. Pratt died suddenly in her bed a few

- **to agree that** = être d'accord pour dire que
- **something the matter with her heart** = une maladie cardiaque
- **It's common enough.** = C'est assez courant.
- **both** = tous les deux
- **There was trouble enough about** = Il y a eu assez de problèmes autour de
- **an inquest** = une enquête
- **the throat** = la gorge
- **to rob** = voler
- **to come to one's end** = mourir
- **teeth** = les dents
- **unknown** = inconnu
- **lay (lie, lay, lain)** = reposait

- **the upper jaw** = la mâchoire du haut
- **no lower one** = pas de mâchoire inférieure

- **set it on** = put it on
- **the shelf** = l'étagère

- **a fisherman** = un pêcheur
- **beside** = à côté

- **what conclusion I reached** = à quelle conclusion je suis arrivé
- **none** = aucune
- **uncomfortable** = mal à l'aise
- **to bother** = tracasser

days after I told that story at dinner. Luke got the doctor over and they agreed that she had died of something the matter with her heart. Why not? It's common enough.

Now they are both dead, and their son, too. There was trouble enough about Luke's death, as it was. How? He was found dead on the beach one morning, and there was an inquest. There were marks on his throat, but he had not been robbed. The verdict was that he had come to his end "by the hands or teeth of some person or animal unknown." He was found lying on his back and an old box that had belonged to his wife lay under his hand, open.

He seemed to have been carrying a skull in the box—doctors are fond of collecting such things. It had rolled out and lay near his head, and it was a remarkably fine skull, rather small and very white, with perfect teeth. That is to say, the upper jaw was perfect, but there was no lower one at all, when I first saw it.

Yes, I found it here when I came. People put it back into the box and set it on the shelf of the cupboard in the best bedroom, and of course they showed it to me when I took possession.

I was taken down to the beach, too, to the place where Luke was found, and the old fisherman explained just how he was lying, and the skull beside him.

You naturally want to know what conclusion I reached, don't you? None. But I got something else into my head, after a time, that made me feel uncomfortable. Oh, I don't mean anything supernatural! No. What bothered

- **foolish** = idiot
- **it occured to me that** = l'idée m'est venue que
- **might** = il se pouvait bien que
- **hers** = le sien (féminin > à elle)
- **there's no sense in that** = c'est absurde

- **all the same** = pourtant
- **convinced** = convaincu

- **to dig (dug, dug) up** = déterrer
- **a lump of lead** = un morceau de plomb

- **I may be all wrong** = Il se peut que je me trompe complètement

- **to give up** = cesser

- **to start** = tressauter

me was just a foolish idea. I was thinking about Luke and his poor wife one evening when it occurred to me that the skull might possibly be hers.

You'll tell me there's no sense in it and that it's perfectly monstrous to suppose her husband kept her skull in his bedroom. All the same, I'm convinced that he did.

Then, don't you see? He killed her, and did it in the same way the woman killed her husbands in the story. They dug up the three skulls, you know, and there was a small lump of lead in each one. That was what hanged the woman. Luke remembered that, I'm sure.

First I tell you that I don't want to know what happened, and that I hate to think about horrors, and then I describe the whole thing to you as if I had seen it. I may be all wrong about the skull, and I like to think that I am when I can.

There! Lord, what a shriek! I told you so! You're quite pale, man. Take some more drink.

Ghosts? No! But it's something that hears and understands; there's no doubt about that.

I tried sleeping in the best bedroom when I first came to the house just because it was the best and most comfortable but I had to give it up. It was their room, and there's the big bed she died in, and the cupboard is in the wall on the left. I felt that something started in the cupboard and the sound inside my head waked me suddenly.

- **afterwards** = ensuite
- **would wake me** = me réveillait fréquemment

- **a fortnight** = deux semaines
- **to grab** = saisir
- **to throw (threw, thrown)** = jeter
- **as far as** = aussi loin que
- **my hair stood on end** = mes cheveux se dressèrent sur ma tête
- **to fall (fell, fallen)** = tomber
- **beyond** = au-delà

- **came nearer and nearer** = se rapprochaient

- **dawn** = l'aube
- **to knock** = frapper à la porte

- **a candle** = une bougie

- **rolled across the threshold** = franchit le seuil en roulant

- **to pick up** = ramasser
- **the shadow** = l'ombre
- **the hollows of the eyes** = les orbites

- **went out** = s'éteignit

That was the first night, and the same thing happened again and several times afterwards. The noise in the cupboard would wake me.

After about a fortnight I had had enough of the noises. One night I got up, and opened the cupboard, grabbed the box and threw it out of the window, as far as I could. Then my hair stood on end. The thing screamed in the air. It fell on the other side of the road. The night was very dark, and I could not see it fall, but I know it fell beyond the road.

I did not sleep much more that night. Half an hour after I had thrown the box out I heard a shriek outside—like what we've had tonight, but worse, more despairing; and the screams came nearer and nearer each time.

A little before dawn someone knocked at the front door. I called out, asking who was there, but nobody answered, though the knock was repeated.

So I took my candle and went down to open the door. There was nobody there, but as I opened the door, something rolled across the threshold and stopped against my foot.

I knew what it was before I looked down.

I shut the door, picked the thing up carefully, and put it on the table beside the candle. The light and shadow from the candle played in the hollows of the eyes as it stood on the table, so that they seemed to open and shut at me. Then the candle went out quite unexpectedly. I sat down rather suddenly, badly frightened. The thing

- **still** = sans bouger
- **to stare** = regardement fixement
- **till** = jusqu'à ce que

- **the hedge** = la haie

- **to lock up** = enfermer

- **missing** = qui manquent
- **the lower jaw** = la mâchoire du bas

- **maybe it fitted that skull** = peut-être qu'elle allait avec ce crâne
- **to stick (stuck, stuck)** = coller

- **no one would find him out** = personne ne le démasquerait
- **to fetch** = aller chercher

- **to start** = sursauter

had come home, and it wanted to go upstairs, back to its cupboard. I sat still and stared at it for a bit till I began to feel very cold; then I took it and carried it up and set it in its place.

When the dawn came, I put on my boots and went out to find the box. I found it on the other side of the hedge. That's all. I took the box upstairs to the cupboard, and put the skull back and locked it up. I moved downstairs that day, and I have never tried to sleep in the best bedroom since.

You think you would like to see the skull? I've no objection. You never saw a more perfect skull in your life, except that there are two front teeth missing in the lower jaw.

Oh yes—I had not told you about the jaw yet. It was James Trehearn who found it in the garden last spring. He brought it to me and asked me if I wanted to keep it. "Maybe it fitted that skull that used to be in the cupboard upstairs, sir," he said. "There's some human hair sticking to it, sir."

What is awful to think of, is Luke's deliberation, if he did it; his cool certainty that no one would find him out.

I'll go upstairs and fetch the box in a minute. Let me light my pipe; there's no hurry! We had supper early, and it's only half-past nine o'clock.

A thing happened that made me start a little when I found that the jaw fitted exactly. Well, just when I had set the jaw in its place under the skull, the teeth closed

- **sharply** = brusquement
- **to bite (bit, bitten)** = mordre
- **to jump** = sursauter
- **queer** = étrange
- **somehow** = d'une certaine façon

- **what rattles about inside** = ce qui bouge et fait du bruit à l'intérieur
- **you had better / I had better** = vous feriez mieux / je ferais mieux de

- **don't let it go out, if you can help it** = ne la laissez pas s'éteindre, si vous le pouvez
- **gale** = tempête

sharply on my finger. It felt exactly as if it were biting me hard. I jumped before I realized that I had been pressing the jaw and the skull together with my other hand. It really made me feel queer. Somehow it made me think of the funny verdict of the coroner's jury on Luke's death, "by the hand or teeth of some person or animal unknown."

Do you suppose that what rattles about inside is really a bit of lead? Well, I'll go upstairs now and get it. What? You had better go with me? Ha, ha! Do you think I'm afraid of a box and a noise? Nonsense!

You think I had better leave you the candle and take the lamp, do you? You may as well finish that glass while I'm getting it.

Here's the box. I brought it down very carefully. Yes, the candle went out as I was coming downstairs. Did you hear anything? Yes, there was another scream. Am I pale, do you say? That's nothing. I went upstairs too fast.

Where did the shriek come from? It was not from the skull, for I had the box in my hand when I heard the noise, and here it is now; the screams are produced by something else.

Now I'll open the box, and we'll take it out and look at it under the bright light.

Take the lamp—don't let it go out, if you can help it. What a gale! There, it's out! I told you so! Never mind, there's the firelight—I've got the window shut. Now,

- **glasses** = lunettes
- **your own** = les vôtres

- **empty** = vide

- **utterly** = tout à fait

- **either of us** = ni l'un ni l'autre

- **awful agony** = horrible torture
- **think of having boiling lead poured** = imaginez que l'on vous verse du plomb brûlant
- **the brain** = le cerveau

- **to faint** = s'évanouir
- **a shroud** = un linceul
- **to be done** = à faire

where's the box? Yes, put it back on the table, and we'll open it.

I'm so glad we heard that last scream together, with the skull here on the table between us, for a thing cannot possibly be in two places at the same time.

Look here, please. Will you take my glasses? No, you have your own. All right.

What! Nothing in it! Empty! It's gone, man, the skull is gone! It's so strange. I'm positively certain that it was inside when I put the box in the cupboard last spring. I can't have imagined that: it's utterly impossible.

The box is empty. We are not dreaming, either of us. There, I turn it upside down. What's that? Something fell out as I turned it over. It's on the floor, it's near your feet. Help me to find it, man. Have you got it? For God's sake, give it to me, quickly! Lead! I knew it when I heard it fall. I knew it. So it was lead after all and Luke did it. He gave her something to make her sleep, of course, but there must have been one moment of awful agony. Think of having boiling lead poured into your brain. Think of it. She was dead before she could scream, but only think of–oh! there it is again—it's just outside—I know it's just outside—I can't keep it out of my head!—oh!—oh!

You thought I had fainted? No. You're as white as a shroud yourself. There's only one thing to be done. We must find it and put it back into its box and shut it up in the cupboard. It wants to get in again. That's why it screams so awfully tonight–it was never so bad as this.

- **to bury** = enterrer

- **I'm losing my senses** = je perds la tête
- **I must get hold of myself** = je dois me reprendre

- **roughly** = brutalement
- **to bite (bit, bitten)** = mordre
- **to bleed (bled, bled)** = saigner
- **carbolic solution** = un antiseptique
- **a drop** = une goutte
- **ghastly** = épouvantable

- **to put away** = ranger

Bury it? Yes, if we can find it, we'll bury it. We'll bury it so deep that it shall never get out again. Quick, we'll get the lantern and look for it. It cannot be far away; I'm sure it's just outside. I know it. Yes, you're quite right. I'm losing my senses, and I must get hold of myself. Don't speak to me for a minute or two; I'll sit quite still and keep my eyes shut.

Hark! What's that knocking? Do you hear it? Knock—knock—knock—three times, then a pause, and then again. It has come home. I've heard that knock before. It wants to come in and be taken upstairs in its box. It's at the front door.

Will you come with me? We'll take it in. Yes, I don't like to go alone and open the door. That's right, come along! I'll take the box with me. Do you hear the knocking? The thing knows we are coming—hark! It's impatient to get in. Don't shut the door till the lantern is ready, whatever you do. Do you hear the knocking still? Here goes—I'll open the door—now! Catch it! Have you got it? The box is on the table. There! Why did you throw it into the box so roughly? It doesn't like that, you know. What do you say? Bitten your hand? Nonsense, man! Let me see. Your finger is bleeding. I'll give you some carbolic solution for it before we go to bed. Just let me see the thing. Ugh! There's a drop of blood on the upper jaw. Ghastly, isn't it?

We'll take it upstairs and put it away where it wants to be. I shall lock the cupboard and keep the key in my pocket. Now we can take the lantern and go upstairs. Yes—this is the door of the best bedroom. Hold up the lantern, please. This side, by the head of the bed. I left

- **will hang about [...] for years** = peut persister

- **the Penraddon News** = un journal local

- **retired** = retraité
- **much disturbed** = très perturbé

- **at once** = aussitôt
- **a practitioner** = un médecin
- **the deceased** = le défunt
- **an assaillant** = un agresseur
- **plainly** = clairement
- **evidently** = manifestement

- **a surgeon** = un médecin / chirurgien

- **a widower** = un veuf

the cupboard open when I got the box. Isn't it queer how the faint odour of women's dresses will hang about an old closet for years? This is the shelf. You've seen me set the box there, and now you see me turn the key and put it into my pocket. So that's done!

Goodnight. Are you sure you're quite comfortable? Goodnight again, and don't dream about that thing, if you can.

The following paragraph appeared in the *Penraddon News,* 23rd November 1906:

MYSTERIOUS DEATH OF A RETIRED SEA CAPTAIN

The village of Tredcombe is much disturbed by the strange death of Captain Charles Braddock. The retired captain was found dead in his bed on Tuesday morning in his own cottage. An examination was made at once by the local practitioner. It revealed the horrible fact that the deceased had been bitten in the throat by a human assailant. The marks of the teeth were so plainly visible on the skin that they could be counted. The assailant had evidently lost two lower front teeth.

The Jury returned the verdict that Captain Braddock came to his death "by the hands or teeth of some person unknown." The local surgeon privately expressed the opinion that the maniac is a woman. Captain Braddock was a widower, and lived alone. He leaves no children.

~

Les 20 mots clés de l'histoire

(to ask) whether = (demander) si
a ship (féminin > she) = un navire
the porthole / the port = le hublot
a ghost = un fantôme
to throw (threw, thrown) = jeter
overboard = par dessus bord
slippery = glissant
to wrestle = lutter
a must read = à lire absolument
a sailor = un marin
the surgeon = le médecin
the deck = le pont (d'un bateau)
in one hundred and five = dans la cabine numéro cent-cinq
the upper / lower berth = la couchette du haut / du bas
flooded = inondé
drowned = noyé
to lock = verrouiller
to doze off = s'assoupir
to shudder = frissonner de peur
to frighten = effrayer

The Deadly Voyage

La traversée mortelle

"*People are always asking whether anybody has seen a ghost. I have.*"

The story is set on a ship on the open sea, which adds an extra element to the horror.

What is going on in cabin 105? The porthole opens in the night with no reason. Several passengers have already thrown themselves overboard through that port. What is that "*slippery, horrible thing*" *Mr*. Brisbane is wrestling with?

A must read for all horror fans, young and old.

The story was originally titled *The Upper Berth* and was first published in 1894. It is one of the most famous ghost stories of the 19th century.

~

- **the guests** = les invités
- **speedily** = rapidement

- **to be bored** = s'ennuyer
- **to be tired** = être fatigué

- **towards** = en direction de
- **the speaker** = celui qui parlait
- **a man of five-and-thirty** = un homme de trente-cinq ans
- **stout** = corpulent
- **thin** = maigre

- **singular** = singulière

- **loud** = forte
- **cutting like a knife** = aussi tranchante qu'un couteau
- **lit** = alluma

- **Bosh!** = N'importe quoi !

- **duck-pond** = marre aux canards (ici, l'Atlantique)

- **luggage** = bagages
- **to mingle** = se mêler

I.

Somebody asked for the cigars. We had talked long; it was already perfectly evident that we, the guests, would speedily go home to bed, and most certainly to sleep. No one had said anything very remarkable; it may be that no one had anything very remarkable to say. We had sat at table for hours; we were bored and we were tired.

Somebody called for cigars. We all instinctively looked towards the speaker. Brisbane was a man of five-and-thirty. He was a strong man. He did not appear to be stout, but, on the other hand, he was certainly not thin and he was in reality very much stronger than he looked. Everybody knows Brisbane, and when he asked for a cigar everybody looked at him.

"It is a very singular thing," said Brisbane.
Everybody stopped talking. Brisbane's voice was not loud, but it was cutting like a knife. Everybody listened. Brisbane, perceiving that he had attracted their general attention, lit his cigar.

"It is very singular," he continued, "that thing about ghosts. People are always asking whether anybody has seen a ghost. I have."
"Bosh! What, you? You don't mean to say so, Brisbane?"
"I am an old sailor," said Brisbane "I have a habit of waiting for certain ships when I am obliged to cross that duck-pond."

"I remember it very well; it was a warm morning in June. I had not much luggage—I never have. I mingled

- **a crowd** = une foule
- **to hasten** = se dépêcher
- **on board** = à bord
- **she no longer is** = il (le bateau, souvent au féminin en anglais) ne l'est plus
- **to hail** = hêler
- **one hundred and five, lower berth** = cabine 105, couchette du bas
- **who think no more of** = qui n'accordent pas plus d'importance
- **a trunk** = une malle
- **I'm d——d!** = I'm damned! = Ç'est pas possible !

- **a mattress** = un matelas
- **a blanket** = une couverture
- **a decanter** = une carafe
- **to fill** = remplir
- **brownish** = brunâtre
- **curtains half-closed the upper-berth** = des rideaux étaient à moitié tirés sur la couchette du haut
- **as if** = comme si
- **to get away** = s'enfuir
- **doubtful** = dubitatif

- **to occur** = avoir lieu
- **sultry** = étouffant

- **lazy** = paresseux
- **amazed** = stupéfait
- **I was to have** = j'allais avoir

with the crowd of passengers. I hastened on board. The *Kamtschatka* was one of my favourite ships. I say was, because she emphatically no longer is. I cannot imagine making another voyage in her. I got on board. I hailed a steward.

"One hundred and five, lower berth," said I, in the tone of those who think no more of crossing the Atlantic than taking a cocktail.
The steward took my trunk. I shall never forget the expression of his face. "Well, I'm d——d!" said he in a low voice.

One hundred and five was on the port side. There was nothing remarkable about the cabin. There was plenty of room. Upon the mattresses there were several blankets. The glass decanters were filled with brownish water. Curtains half-closed the upper berth. "Ugh! How I hate that cabin!"

The steward deposited my luggage and looked at me, as if he wanted to get away. "I'll try and make as you comfortable as I can," he remarked but there was a doubtful intonation in his voice which surprised me.

II.

Nothing remarkable occurred during that day. The weather was warm and sultry, but there was a refreshing breeze.

On that first night of the voyage I felt particularly lazy, and went to bed rather earlier than I usually do. I was

- **very like my own** = très semblable à la mienne
- **to lie (lay, lain)** = être posé
- **alone** = seul
- **to wonder** = se demander
- **room-mate** = compagnon de chambre

- **over-dressed** = trop bien habillé
- **odd** = bizarre
- **I made up my mind that I did not care to make his acquaintance.** = Je décidai que je n'avais aucune envie de faire sa connaissance.
- **Poor fellow!** = Pauvre garçon !
- **waked** = réveillé
- **must have sprung (spring, sprang, sprung)** = avait dû sauter
- **his footsteps** = ses pas

- **as if he were running for his life** = comme s'il fuyait un danger mortel

- **to awake (awoke, awoken)** = se réveiller
- **damp** = humide
- **to doze off** = s'assoupir
- **while** = pendant que
- **once** = à un moment
- **to groan** = gémir
- **to be sea-sick** = avoir le mal de mer
- **till early daylight** = jusqu'aux premières lueurs du jour

- **wide open** = grand ouvert
- **to glance** = jeter un coup d'œil

amazed to see that I was to have a companion. A trunk, very like my own, lay in the opposite corner. I had hoped to be alone, and I was disappointed; but I wondered who my room-mate was to be, and I determined to have a look at him.

Before I had been long in bed he entered. He was a very tall man, very thin, very pale, with grey eyes. He was the sort of man who frequents the Café Anglais, who always seems to be alone and who drinks champagne, a little over-dressed—a little odd. I made up my mind that I did not care to make his acquaintance. Poor fellow! I never saw him again after that first night in one hundred and five.

I was sleeping when I was suddenly waked by a loud noise. My room-mate must have sprung from the upper berth to the floor. I heard his footsteps as he ran down the passage, leaving the door open behind him. He ran as if he were running for his life. I got up and shut it. I went to sleep again; but I have no idea how long I slept.

When I awoke it was still quite dark, but I felt a disagreeable sensation of cold, and it seemed to me that the air was damp. I covered myself up as well as I could and dozed off again. I could hear my room-mate turn over in the upper berth. He had probably returned while I was asleep. Once I thought I heard him groan, and I thought that he was sea-sick. I dozed off and slept till early daylight.

It was very cold. I turned my head and looked at the porthole, and saw to my surprise that it was wide open. Then I got up and shut it. As I turned back I glanced at

- **the curtains were drawn close together** = les rideaux été complètement tirés
- **as well as I** = comme moi
- **it struck me (strike, struck, struck/stricken)** = j'eus l'impression
- **though** = bien que
- **to smell** = sentir
- **the dampness** = l'humidité
- **to avoid** = éviter
- **at once** = aussitôt
- **on deck** = sur le pont
- **to come across (came, come)** = tomber sur
- **a tremendous fellow** = un homme incroyable
- **he had a healthy look about him** = il respirait la santé

- **however** = cependant
- **to notice** = remarquer

- **to start** = sursauter
- **to stare** = regarder fixement
- **to complain** = se plaindre
- **the last three trips** = les trois derniers voyages
- **properly** = correctement
- **to air** = aérer
- **I don't think it can be helped** = je ne pense pas qu'on y puisse grand-chose
- **it is not my business** = je ne suis pas censé
- **to frighten** = faire peur
- **you need not be afraid of** = ne craignez pas de
- **If I should get a bad cold** =si jamais je prenais froid

the upper berth. The curtains were drawn close together; my companion had probably felt cold as well as I.
It struck me that I had slept enough. The cabin was uncomfortable, though I could not smell the dampness which had annoyed me in the night. My room-mate was still asleep—excellent opportunity for avoiding him, so I dressed at once and went on deck.

The day was warm and cloudy. I came across the doctor. He was a young man from the West of Ireland—a tremendous fellow, with black hair and blue eyes, he had a healthy look about him which was rather attractive.

"Fine morning," I remarked.
"Well," said he, "it's a fine morning and it's not a fine morning."
"Well, no—it is not so very fine," said I, "it was very cold last night, I thought," I remarked. "However, I found that the porthole was wide open. I had not noticed it when I went to bed. And the cabin was damp, too."
"Damp!" said he. "Where are you?"
"One hundred and five——"
To my surprise the doctor started and stared at me.
"What is the matter?" I asked.
"Oh—nothing," he answered; "only everybody has complained of that cabin for the last three trips."
"I shall complain too," I said. "It has certainly not been properly aired. It is a shame!"
"I don't believe it can be helped," answered the doctor. "I believe there is something—well, it is not my business to frighten passengers."
"You need not be afraid of frightening me," I replied. "If I should get a bad cold I will come to you."
I offered the doctor a cigar.

- **to share** = partager

- **advice** = conseils
- **I'd rather see you overboard** = Je préfèrerais vous voir passer par-dessus bord
- **than have you sleep** = que vous laisser dormir

- **actually** = réellement

- **to make game of** = se moquer de

- **to whisper** = chuchoter

"It is not so much the damp," he remarked. "Have you a room-mate?"
"Yes a fellow, who runs out in the middle of the night and leaves the door open."
Again the doctor glanced curiously at me.
"Did he come back?" he asked.
"Yes. I was asleep, but I waked up and heard him moving. Then I felt cold and went to sleep again. This morning I found the porthole open."
"Look here," said the doctor, quietly, "I have a place up here. I will share it with you." I was very much surprised at the proposition.
"You are very good, doctor," I said. "But really, I believe even now the cabin could be aired."
"I don't want to frighten you, replied the doctor, but if you will take my advice you will move in here. I'd rather see you overboard," he added, "than have you sleep in one hundred and five."
"Why?" I asked.
"Just because on the last three trips the people who have slept there actually have gone overboard," he answered, gravely.

The news was exceedingly unpleasant, I confess. I looked at the doctor to see whether he was making game of me, but he looked perfectly serious. I thanked him warmly for his offer, but told him I intended to be the exception to the rule. He did not say much, but looked very grave. After breakfast I went into my cabin. The curtains of the upper berth were still closely drawn. My room-mate was probably still asleep.

As I came out I met the steward. He whispered that the captain wanted to see me. I went toward the captain's

- **to stagger** = décontenancer

- **I fear he has** = j'ai bien peur que si

- **the fourth** = le quatrième

- **to find (found, found)** = retrouver
- **to lose (lost, lost)** = perdre (en mer)

- **a bad name** = mauvaise réputation
- **any** = n'importe laquelle
- **my own** = la mienne
- **obliged** = reconnaissant.
- **since** = puisque
- **to myself** = pour moi tout seul
- I **would rather** = je préfèrerais

- **I wish you would let me** = laissez-moi

cabin, and found him waiting for me.
"Sir, your room-mate has disappeared," he said. "Did you notice anything extraordinary?"
The question staggered me.
"You don't mean to say he has gone overboard?" I asked.
"I fear he has," answered the captain.
"This is the most extraordinary thing——" I began.
"Why?" he asked.
"He is the fourth, then?" I explained. I explained that I had heard the story concerning one hundred and five. He seemed very much annoyed. I told him what had occurred in the night.
"What you say," he replied, "coincides almost exactly with what was told me by the room-mates of two of the other three. They jump out of bed and run down the passage. Two of them were seen to go overboard; we stopped, but they were not found. Nobody, however, saw or heard the man who was lost last night—if he is really lost. Now, sir, do not mention the circumstance to any of the passengers; I don't want the ship to get a bad name. You shall have your choice of any one of the officers' cabins you like, including my own, for the rest of the passage."
"I am much obliged to you. But since I am alone, and have the cabin to myself, I would rather not move. I think I can promise you that I will not follow my room-mate."
The captain tried to dissuade me from my intention, but I preferred having a cabin alone.
"Of course you have a right to stay where you are," he replied; "but I wish you would let me lock the place up."

- **to change one's mind** = changer d'avis

- **I could not help** = je ne pouvais pas m'empêcher de
- **previous** = précédent(e)
- **drowned** = noyé
- **I became aware (become, became)** = je me rendis compte
- **to stand** = supporter

- **to drag** = emmener de force

- **to leave (left, left)** = laisser
- **the regulations** = le règlement

- **perfectly tight** = hermétiquement fermé

- **roused** = réveillé

I did not see it in the same light, and left the captain. Towards evening I met the doctor again, and he asked me whether I had changed my mind. I told him I had not.
"Then you will before long," he said, very gravely.

III.

I went to bed late. I will confess now that I felt a disagreeable sensation when I entered my cabin. I could not help thinking of the tall man I had seen on the previous night, who was now dead, drowned. I locked the door of the cabin. Suddenly I became aware that the porthole was open. This was more than I could stand. I went in search of Robert, the steward. I was very angry, I remember, and when I found him I dragged him to the door of one hundred and five, and pushed him towards the open porthole.
"What do you mean by leaving that porthole open every night? Don't you know it is against the regulations?"
The man trembled and turned pale, and then began to shut the porthole.
"Why don't you answer me?" I said.
"If you please, sir," said Robert, "there's nobody on board who can keep this porthole shut at night. If I was you, sir, I'd just go and sleep with the surgeon."
I tried the porthole, and found it perfectly tight.
Robert walked away. Of course I did not believe him.

I went to bed and tried to go to sleep, but I soon found that impossible. I was just dozing into sleep when I was roused by the cold air. The porthole was again wide open! Now these things are facts. The porthole was wide open. I at once closed it again. I must have

- **to remain** = rester

- **a faint groan** = un faible gémissement
- **I tore (tear, tore, torn) ... aside** = j'ouvris violemment

- **I laid hold of (lay, laid, laid)** = j'attrapai
- **the shape** = la forme
- **smooth** = lisse
- **icy cold** = glacial
- **to pull** = tirer
- **sprang [...] forward against me** = se jeta sur moi
- **yet** = et pourtant
- **strength** = force
- **to rush out** = s'enfuit précipitamment
- **a shadow** = une ombre
- **to be ashamed** = avoir honte
- **Still I doubted my senses.** = Cependant je doutais de ce que j'avais vu.
- **a nightmare** = un cauchemar

- **creeping** = insidieuse

- **the bed had been slept in** = quelqu'un avait bien dormi dans le lit
- **as dry as a bone** = sec comme un os

- **to recover my senses** = pour reprendre mes esprits

remained there a quarter of an hour. Suddenly, as I stood, I distinctly heard something moving behind me in one of the berths, and just as I turned instinctively to look, I heard a very faint groan. I tore the curtains of the upper berth aside to discover if there were any one there.

There was some one. I laid hold of something that had the shape of a man's arm, but was smooth, and wet, and icy cold. But suddenly, as I pulled, the creature sprang violently forward against me, heavy and wet, yet with a sort of supernatural strength. In an instant the door opened and the thing rushed out. I had not had time to be frightened, I sprang through the door but I was too late. I am sure I saw it—a dark shadow moving. But in a moment it had disappeared. I am not ashamed of it: I was very badly frightened.

Still I doubted my senses. It was absurd, I thought. I had been in a nightmare. I went back to my cabin, and entered it. The whole place smelled of stagnant sea-water. As I lighted a lantern, I perceived that the porthole was again open, and a sort of creeping horror began to take possession of me. But I got a light and examined the upper berth.

I was disappointed. The bed had been slept in, and the smell of the sea was strong; but the bed was as dry as a bone. I drew the curtains back as far as I could and examined the place very carefully. It was perfectly dry. But the porthole was open again.

With horror, I closed it and locked it. Then I sat down to recover my senses if I could. I sat there all night, unable

- **unable** = incapable

- **to dawn** = se lever (le jour)

- **I am likely to doubt the story** = je pourrais douter de votre histoire

- **the bottom of** = le fond de

- **it is my business to keep my wits about me** = il est de mon devoir de garder la tête froide
- **to fiddle about with** = se mêler de

- **rather contempluously** = avec un certain mépris

to think. But the porthole remained closed.

The morning dawned at last, and I dressed myself slowly, thinking over all that had happened in the night. It was a beautiful day and I went on deck, glad to get out. Instinctively I turned towards the surgeon's cabin.
"Good-morning," said he looking at me with evident curiosity.
"Doctor, you were quite right," said I. "There is something wrong about that place."
"I thought you would change your mind," he answered, rather triumphantly. "You have had a bad night, eh?"
I cried : "But I would like to tell you what happened."
I then tried to explain as clearly as possible precisely what had occurred.
"You seem to think I am likely to doubt the story," said the doctor. "I do not doubt it. Take half my cabin."
"Come and take half of mine for one night," I said. "Help me to get at the bottom of this thing."
"You will get to the bottom of something else if you try," answered the doctor.
"What?" I asked.
"The bottom of the sea. I am going to leave the ship."
"Then you will not help me to find out—"
"Not I," said the doctor, quickly. "It is my business to keep my wits about me—not to go fiddling about with ghosts and things."
"Do you really believe it is a ghost?" I inquired, rather contemptuously. But as I spoke I remembered very well the horrible sensation of the supernatural which had got possession of me during the night.
"Have you any reasonable explanation of these things to offer?" he asked. "No; you have not. Well, you say you will find an explanation. I say that you won't, sir,

- **to retort** = rétorquer

- **I did not care to** = je n'avais pas envie de

- **I will share your watch myself** = je monterai moi-même la garde avec vous
- **some fellow [...] who steals a passage** = un type qui voyage clandestinement

- **a ghastly grin** = un rictus effroyable
- **my spirits had risen** = j'avais de nouveau le moral
- **at the prospect of** = à l'idée de

- **we went below** = nous descendîmes

simply because there is not any."
"But, my dear sir," I retorted, "do you, a man of science, mean to tell me that such things cannot be explained?"
"I do," he answered.
I did not care to spend another night alone in the cabin.
A little later I met the captain, and told him my story.
"Look here," said he, "I will tell you what I will do. I will share your watch myself, and we will see what happens. There may be some fellow on board, who steals a passage by frightening the passengers. There may be something queer in that berth."

We examined the place. Everything was in perfect order. As we were finishing our work, Robert came to the door and looked in.
"Well, sir—find anything, sir?" he asked with a ghastly grin.
My spirits had risen considerably at the prospect of having the captain's company.

IV.

The captain combined courage and calmness. About ten o'clock that evening he came up to me.
"This is a serious matter, Mr. Brisbane," he said. "If nothing happens to-night we will try it again to-morrow and next day. Are you ready?"

So we went below, and entered the cabin. The captain closed the door behind us and locked it.
"Supposing we put your trunk before the door," he suggested. "One of us can sit on it. Nothing can get out then. Is the porthole locked?"

- **either... or...** = soit ... soit...

- **a lunatic** = un fou
- **who had the watch** = qui était de quart
- **his suicide was afterwards accounted for on the grounds of his insanity** = on a ensuite dit que son suicide était à mettre sur le compte de sa démence

- **riveted upon** = rivés sur

- **is supposed to** = est censé

- **flooded** = inondé
- **to manage** = réussir
- **damage** = des dégâts

I found it as I had left it in the morning. No one could have opened it. I drew back the curtains of the upper berth so that I could see well into it.

"It is impossible for any human being to get in," I said, "or for any human being to open the port."

"Very good," said the captain, calmly. "If we see anything now, it must be either imagination or something supernatural."

I sat down on the lower berth.

"The first time it happened," said the captain, crossing his legs "was in March. The passenger who slept here, in the upper berth, must have been a lunatic. He rushed out in the middle of the night, and threw himself overboard, before the officer who had the watch could stop him. We stopped; it was a quiet night but we could not find him. Of course his suicide was afterwards accounted for on the ground of his insanity."

"I suppose that often happens?" I remarked.

"Not often—no," said the captain; "never before in my experience. On the very next trip—what are you looking at?" he asked, stopping suddenly in his narration.

I believe I gave no answer. My eyes were riveted upon the porthole. Seeing where I was looking, the captain looked too.

"It moves!" he exclaimed, in a tone of conviction. "No, it does not," he added, after a minute.

"The queer thing," said the captain, "is that the second man who was lost is supposed to have got through that very porthole. It was in the middle of the night; there was an alarm that one of the portholes was open and the sea running in. I came below and found everything flooded. Well, we managed to shut the porthole, but the water did some damage. Ever since that the place smells of sea-water from time to time. We supposed the

- **ever since that** = depuis lors

- **to shudder** = frissonner de peur

- **He was wrestling with the loop of the port.** = Il se débattait avec la poignée du hublot.

- **it shall not escape us, whatever it is** = cette chose ne nous échappera pas, quelle qu'elle soit

- **ghostly** = fantomatique
- **long drowned** = noyé depuis longtemps
- **to grip** = agripper
- **slippery** = glissant

- **the [...] odour [...] was about it** = elle (la chose) sentait
- **its hair hung (hang, hung, hung)** = ses cheveux pendaient
- **to thrust (thrust, thrust) upon** = se jeter sur
- **to wind (wound, wound)** = enrouler
- **to overpower** = prendre le dessus

- **he struck a violent blow (strike, struck, struck)** = il frappa violemment

passenger had thrown himself out. I can smell it now, cannot you?" he inquired.
"Yes—distinctly," I said, and I shuddered.

My reading-lantern was suddenly extinguished. I rose quickly from my seat, and the captain at the same moment gave a loud cry of surprise. I sprang towards him. He was wrestling with the loop of the porthole. It seemed to turn against his hands in spite of all his efforts. I fell upon the couch. When I rose again the porthole was wide open, and the captain was standing with his back against the door, pale to the lips.
"There is something in that berth!" he cried, in a strange voice. "Hold the door, while I look—it shall not escape us, whatever it is!"

But instead of taking his place, I sprang upon the lower bed, and seized something which lay in the upper berth. It was something ghostly, horrible and it moved. It was like the body of a man long drowned, and yet it moved, and had the strength of ten men living; but I gripped it the slippery, horrible thing.

The dead white eyes seemed to stare at me; the putrid odour of sea-water was about it, and its hair hung over its dead face. I wrestled with the dead thing; it thrust itself upon me and nearly broke my arms; it wound its arms about my neck, the living death, and overpowered me, so that I, at last, cried aloud and fell.

As I fell the thing seemed to throw itself upon the captain. When I last saw him on his feet his face was white. It seemed to me that he struck a violent blow at the dead being, and then he, too, fell forward upon his

- **the dead being** = l'être mort

- **to hover** = plâner
- **to vanish** = disparaître

- **more than any one can tell** = impossible à dire

- **my remaining hand** = l'autre main
- **to raise** = soulever
- **came to himself** = revint à lui
- **hurt** = blessé
- **badly stunned** = très choqué

- **to doctor** = soigner
- **to advise** = conseiller

- **anyhow** = en tout cas

face, with an inarticulate cry of horror.

The thing paused an instant, seeming to hover over the body. The thing vanished suddenly, and it seemed to me that it went through the open porthole, though how that was possible is more than any one can tell. I lay a long time upon the floor. At last I moved, and I instantly knew that my arm was broken. I got upon my feet, and with my remaining hand I tried to raise the captain. He groaned and moved, and at last came to himself. He was not hurt, but he seemed badly stunned.

Well, do you want to hear any more? There is nothing more. That is the end of my story. I finished the trip in the surgeon's cabin. He doctored my broken arm, and advised me not to "fiddle about with ghosts and things" any more. The captain was very silent, and never sailed again in that ship. And I will not sail in her either. It was a very disagreeable experience, and I was very badly frightened, which is a thing I do not like. That is all. That is how I saw a ghost—if it was a ghost. It was dead, anyhow."

~

SAKI (Hector Hugh Munro)

(1870–1916) is a famous British writer and a master of the short story form. Many of his stories are characterized by humour and satire, while some of his tales are truly terrifying. Saki is regarded as one of the greatest short story writers. His stories were initially published in newspapers and later collected into several volumes. Saki's plays and stories have also been adapted as TV series.

Les 10 mots clés de l'histoire

wild = sauvage

a beast = une bête

the game = le gibier

the lambs and poultry = les agneaux et la volaille

reported missing = porté disparu

naked / nude = nu

flesh = la chair

a youngster = un jeune garçon

a shriek = un cri perçant

at sunset = au coucher de soleil

Gabriel Ernest

"There is a wild beast in your woods."

Something is killing the game. The lambs and poultry are mysteriously disappearing. A young child has been reported missing.

Who is the beautiful naked boy living in the woods who turns up in the narrator's home?

Gabriel Ernest is the perfect "H" story: "H" for **H**orror and... **H**umour.

~

- **the drive** = le trajet (en voiture)

- **his aunt had possibly some justification in** = sa tante n'avait peut-être pas tout à fait tort de
- **custom** = habitude
- **to provide** = fournir
- **topics for conversation** = des sujets de conversation

- **however** = cependant
- **far removed** = très éloigné
- **on a stone overhanging a pool** = sur une dalle de pierre surplombant une pièce d'eau
- **to dry** = sécher
- **his (...) eyes had a tigerish gleam in them =** ses yeux luisaient comme ceux d'un tigre
- **unexpected** = inattendue
- **mill / miller** = moulin / meunier

- **to drown** = se noyer
- **a mere baby** = un tout petit enfant
- **half-grown** = adolescent
- **obviously** = de toute évidence
- **to sun oneself** = prendre le soleil

"There is a wild beast in your woods," said Cunningham, as he was being driven to the station. It was the only remark he had made during the drive and Van Cheele had talked incessantly.

"What did you mean about a wild beast?" said Van Cheele later, when they were on the platform.
"Nothing. My imagination. Here is the train," said Cunningham.

That afternoon Van Cheele went for a walk through his property. He knew the names of a number of wild flowers, so his aunt had possibly some justification in describing him as a great naturalist. At any rate, he was a great walker. It was his custom to take mental notes of everything he saw during his walks, to provide topics for conversation afterwards.

What Van Cheele saw on this particular afternoon was, however, something far removed from his experience.

On a stone overhanging a pool, a boy of about sixteen was drying luxuriously in the sun. His hair was wet and his brown eyes had a tigerish gleam in them; they were turned towards Van Cheele.

It was an unexpected apparition. Where on earth could this wild-looking boy come from? The miller's wife had lost a child some two months ago, who was supposed to have drowned, but that had been a mere baby, not a half-grown boy.

"What are you doing there?" he demanded.
"Obviously, sunning myself," replied the boy.

- **patronage** = condescendance

- **busy** = occupé

- **relish** = délectation

- **too well locked in** = trop bien protégés dans leur maison (= sous clé)
- **hunting/ to hunt** = la chasse / chasser
- **it's quite two months since I tasted** = cela fait deux mois que je n'ai pas mangé de
- **poaching** = le braconnage
- **a hare** = un lièvre
- **to catch (caught, caught)** = attraper

- **weird** = étrange
- **both** = à la fois

- **uncanny** = troublant
- **I can't have you staying** = je ne peux vous autoriser à rester

- **I think you'd rather have me here than…** = je pense qu'il est préférable pour vous que je sois ici plutôt que…

"Where do you live?"
"Here, in these woods."
"You can't live in the woods," said Van Cheele.
"They are very nice woods," said the boy, with a touch of patronage in his voice.
"But where do you sleep at night?"
"I don't sleep at night; that's my busiest time."
Van Cheele began to feel irritated.
"What do you feed on?" he asked.
"Flesh," said the boy, and he pronounced the word with relish.
"Flesh! What flesh?"
"Since it interests you, rabbits, poultry, lambs, children when I can get any; they're usually too well locked in at night, when I do most of my hunting. It's quite two months since I tasted child-flesh."

Ignoring the mockery, Van Cheele tried to draw the boy on the subject of poaching.
"Our hares aren't easily caught."
"At night I hunt on four feet," was the cryptic response.
"I suppose you mean that you hunt with a dog?" hazarded Van Cheele.

The boy rolled slowly over on to his back, and laughed a weird laugh that was both pleasant and disagreeable.
"I don't think any dog would want my company, especially at night."
Van Cheele began to feel that there was something positively uncanny about the youngster.
"I can't have you staying in these woods," he declared authoritatively.
"I think you'd rather have me here than in your house," said the boy.

- **the prospect** = l'idée

- **I shall have to make you** = je serai contraint de vous y obliger
- **a flash** = un éclair
- **was half-way up the bank** = était remonté à mi-hauteur de la berge
- **startled** = stupéfait
- **to slip** = glisser
- **prostrate** = à plat ventre
- **the throat** = la gorge
- **to plunge out of view** = disparaître

- **picked himself up** = se relevait
- **to recall** = se rappeler

- **to turn things over in his mind** = réfléchir

- **lately** = ces derniers temps
- **to carry off** = enlever

- **poacher dogs** = des chiens de braconnage
- **"four-footed"** = sur quatre pattes
- **puzzling =** déconcertant

- **to come to a dead stop** = s'arrêter net

- **uncanny** = troublante

The prospect of this wild, nude animal in Van Cheele's well-ordered house was certainly alarming.
"If you don't go, I shall have to make you," said Van Cheele.
The boy turned like a flash, plunged into the pool, and in a moment was half-way up the bank where Van Cheele was standing. Van Cheele was startled. His foot slipped and he found himself almost prostrate on the bank, with those tigerish eyes not very far from his own.

Almost instinctively he raised his hand to his throat. The boy laughed again then plunged out of view.
"What an extraordinary wild animal!" said Van Cheele as he picked himself up. And then he recalled Cunningham's remark "There is a wild beast in your woods."

Walking slowly home, Van Cheele began to turn things over in his mind.
Something had been killing the game in the woods lately. Poultry had been missing from the farms and lambs had been carried off. Was it possible that this wild boy was really hunting the countryside with some poacher dogs? He had spoken of hunting "four-footed" by night, but with no dog, "especially at night." It was certainly puzzling.

Van Cheele came suddenly to a dead stop in his speculations. The child missing from the mill two months ago; the mother had always declared she had heard a shriek, in the opposite direction from the water.

It was unthinkable, of course, but the boy had made that uncanny remark about child-flesh eaten two months

- **dreadful** = terrible
- **even in fun** = même pour rire

- **parish councillor and justice of the peace** = conseiller municipal et juge de paix
- **to harbour** = héberger

- **that a heavy bill of damages [...] might be laid at his door** = qu'on lui réclame de lourds dommages et intérêts

- **one would think...** = à croire que...
- **a wolf** = un loup

- **foolish** = idiote

- **uneasiness** = malaise
- **to resolve** = se décider

- **cheerfulness** = gaité
- **to hum** = fredonner
- **customary** = habituelle
- **an ottoman** = un divan

- **noticeable** = remarquable

- **how dare you** = comment osez-vous
- **I was not to stay** = que je ne devais pas

- **supposing** = imaginez que

ago. Such dreadful things should not be said even in fun.

Van Cheele did not feel disposed to talk about his discovery in the wood. He was a parish councillor and justice of the peace. And his position seemed compromised by the fact that he was harbouring such a personality on his property; there was even a possibility that a heavy bill of damages for the lambs and poultry might be laid at his door.

At dinner that night he was quite unusually silent.
"Where's your voice gone to?" said his aunt. "One would think you had seen a wolf."

Van Cheele thought the remark rather foolish; if he *had* seen a wolf on his property he would have talked about it. At breakfast next morning Van Cheele was conscious that his feeling of uneasiness had not disappeared, and he resolved to go by train to consult Cunningham, and learn from him what he had really seen in the woods.

With this resolution taken, his usual cheerfulness partially returned. And he hummed a little melody as he entered the morning-room for his customary cigarette. Gracefully lying on the ottoman in an attitude of almost exaggerated repose, was the boy of the woods. He was drier than when Van Cheele had last seen him, but no other change was noticeable in his toilet.
"How dare you come here?" asked Van Cheele furiously.
"You told me I was not to stay in the woods," said the boy calmly.
"But not to come here. Supposing my aunt should see you!"

- **hastily obscured** = dissimula précipitamment
- **a guest** = un invité
- **the Morning Post** = a daily newspaper

- **perhaps his underlinen is marked** = peut-être que ses sous-vêtements sont marqués à son nom
- **homeless** = abandonné (sans-abri)
- **to appeal to** = avoir de l'attrait
- **a stray kitten** = un petit chat perdu

- **sweet** = adorable
- **call him something** = lui trouver un nom
- **till** = jusqu'à ce que
- **suitable** = convenables

- **to agree** = acquiescer
- **he privately doubted whether** = en son for intérieur, il doutait que

- **to bolt out** = s'enfuir
- **at the first incoming of the boy** = dès l'arrivée du garçon
- **remained shivering** = se tenait tremblant
- **the orchard** = le verger

- **without loss of time** = sans perdre un instant

- **to entertain** = divertir
- **the children of her Sunday-school class** = les enfants de sa classe de l'École du dimanche

And Van Cheele hastily obscured as much of his guest as possible under the *Morning Post*. At that moment his aunt entered the room.
"This is a poor boy who has lost his way—and lost his memory. He doesn't know who he is or where he comes from," explained Van Cheele desperately.
Miss Van Cheele was enormously interested.
"Perhaps his underlinen is marked," she suggested.
"He seems to have lost that, too," said Van Cheele.
A naked homeless child appealed to Miss Van Cheele as warmly as a stray kitten.
"We must do all we can for him," she decided, and in a very short time, the boy was clothed and clean. He did not lose his uncanniness in Van Cheele's eyes. But his aunt found him sweet.
"We must call him something till we know who he really is," she said. "Gabriel-Ernest, I think; those are nice suitable names."

Van Cheele agreed, but he privately doubted whether those names were being given to a nice suitable child.

His apprehension was not diminished by the fact that his dog had bolted out of the house at the first incoming of the boy, and now obstinately remained shivering in the orchard.

More than ever he was resolved to consult Cunningham without loss of time.

As he drove off to the station his aunt said that Gabriel-Ernest would help her to entertain the children of her Sunday-school class at tea that afternoon.

- **brain trouble** = maladie mentale

- **I became aware of** = j'aperçus
- **on the hillside** = sur la colline

- **the landscape** = le paysage
- **astounding** = stupéfiant

- **to vanish** = disparaître

- **dreadful** = terrible

- **blackish** = noirâtre

- **to rush** = se précipiter
- **dismissed** = écarta
- **a werewolf** = un loup-garou
- **a code message to which he had omitted to give her the key** = un message codé dont il avait omis de lui donner la clé
- **his one hope** = son seul espoir
- **to reach** = atteindre
- **to sink** = sombrer
- **to scream** = hurler

Cunningham was not at first disposed to be communicative.
"My mother died of some brain trouble," he explained, "so you will understand why I do not want to talk about anything of a fantastic nature that I may see or think I have seen."
"But what *did* you see?" persisted Van Cheele.
"What I thought I saw was something absolutely extraordinary. I was standing, the last evening I was with you, in the orchard, watching the sunset. Suddenly I became aware of a naked boy on the hillside who was also watching the sunset. Then the sun went out of view, and all the orange and pink disappeared, leaving the landscape cold and grey. And at the same moment an astounding thing happened—the boy vanished too!"

"What! Vanished into nothing?" asked Van Cheele excitedly.
"No; that is the dreadful part of it," answered Cunningham; "on the hillside where the boy had been standing, stood a large wolf, blackish in colour, with cruel, yellow eyes. You may think—"

But Van Cheele did not stop for anything as futile as thought. Already he was rushing towards the station. He dismissed the idea of a telegram saying: "Gabriel-Ernest is a werewolf." His aunt would think it was a code message to which he had omitted to give her the key.

His one hope was that he might reach home before sunset. His aunt was putting away some unfinished jams and cake when he arrived. The sun was sinking.
"Where is Gabriel-Ernest?" he almost screamed.

- **the little Toop child** = le petit de la famille Toop
- **safe** = prudent
- **it** = the child
- **alone** = tout seul
- **to race** = courir à toute vitesse
- **the lane** = le chemin
- **a rim of red sun** = un anneau de soleil rougeoyant
- **a shrill cry** = un cri aigu

- **nothing was ever seen again of** = on ne revit jamais

- **it was assumed** = on supposa
- **to strip** = se dévêtir

- **the spot** = l'endroit

- **resigned to her loss** = résignée à la perte de son enfant
- **sincerely mourned** = pleura sincèrement la mort de
- **a memorial** = un monument commémoratif

- **to give way** = céder
- **flatly refused** = refusa catégoriquement
- **to subscribe** = contribuer financièrement

"He is taking the little Toop child home," said his aunt. "It was getting so late, I thought it wasn't safe to let it go back alone. What a lovely sunset, isn't it?"
But Van Cheele did not stay to discuss the beauties of the sky. He raced along the lane that led to the home of the Toops. There still was a rim of red sun. Then the colour suddenly disappeared and there was a grey light over the landscape. Van Cheele heard a shrill cry of fear, and stopped running.

Nothing was ever seen again of the Toop child or Gabriel-Ernest, but Gabriel-Ernest's clothes were found lying in the road. It was assumed that the child had fallen into the water, and that the boy had stripped and jumped in, to save it.

Van Cheele and some workmen who were nearby declared they had heard a child scream loudly just near the spot where the clothes were found.

Mrs. Toop, who had eleven other children, was decently resigned to her loss.
But Miss Van Cheele sincerely mourned Gabriel-Ernest. It was on her initiative that a memorial was put up in the parish church to "Gabriel-Ernest, an unknown boy, who bravely sacrificed his life for another."

Van Cheele gave way to his aunt in most things, but he flatly refused to subscribe to the Gabriel-Ernest memorial.

~

Les 10 mots clés de l'histoire

wide open = grande ouverte

to stare = regarder fixement

a nervous breakdown = une dépression nerveuse

from Vera's own lips = de la bouche de Vera

to bury = enterrer

shooting = la chasse

the twilight = dusk = le crépuscule

a spaniel = un chien épagneul

a figure = une silhouette

a grave = une tombe

The Open Window

La fenêtre ouverte

"Her great tragedy happened just three years ago." The child was staring out through the open window with horror in her eyes.

Why is the window kept wide open on an October afternoon? Why does Vera's aunt act so strangely? Framton Nuttel, who has moved to the country to recover from a nervous breakdown, will hear all about it from Vera's own lips.

The end is totally unexpected.
This story is pure delight!

~

- **will be down presently** = va descendre dans un instant
- **very self-possessed** = très sûre d'elle
- **in the meantime** = en attendant
- **to put up with** = supporter

- **privately** = en son for intérieur
- **he doubted whether (...) would do much to improve his nervous condition** = il doutait que (...) puissent calmer ses nerfs

- **a living soul** = âme qui vive
- **from moping** = à force de broyer du noir

- **as far as I can remember** = autant que je m'en souvienne

- **hardly a soul** = pratiquement personne
- **at the rectory** = au presbytère
- **some four years ago** = il y a environ quatre ans

- **a statement** = une déclaration

- **the caller** = le visiteur

- **was in the married or widowed state** = était mariée ou veuve
- **an undefinable something** = quelque chose d'indéfinissable

"My aunt will be down presently, Mr. Nuttel," said a very self-possessed young lady of fifteen; "in the meantime you must try and put up with me."

Framton tried to say the correct thing to flatter the niece while waiting for the aunt. Privately he doubted whether these formal visits on total strangers would do much to improve his nervous condition.

"I know how it will be," his sister had said; "you will bury yourself down there and not speak to a living soul, and your nerves will be worse than ever from moping. I shall just give you letters of introduction to all the people I know there. Some of them, as far as I can remember, were quite nice."

"Do you know many of the people round here?" asked the niece, when she judged that they had had sufficient silent communion.

"Hardly a soul," said Framton. "My sister was staying here, at the rectory, you know, some four years ago, and she gave me letters of introduction to some of the people here."

He made the last statement in a tone of regret.

"Then you know practically nothing about my aunt?" pursued the self-possessed young lady.

"Only her name and address," admitted the caller.

He was wondering whether Mrs. Sappleton was in the married or widowed state. An undefinable something

- **about the room** = dans la pièce

- **since your sister's time** = après le départ de votre sœur

- **restful country spot** = dans ce paisible coin de campagne
- **out of place** = pas à leur place

- **French window** = porte-fenêtre
- **to open on to** = donner sur
- **the lawn** = la pelouse
- **anything to do with** = quelque chose à voir avec

- **out through that window** = par cette fenêtre
- **to a day** = jour pour jour
- **their day's shooting** = leur journée de chasse
- **the moor** = la lande
- **engulfed** = engloutis
- **a piece of bog** = un marécage
- **recovered** = retrouvés

- **someday** = un jour

- **as they used to** = comme avant
- **till it is quite dusk** = presque jusqu'au crépuscule

- **to bound** = faire des bonds

about the room seemed to suggest masculine habitation.

"Her great tragedy happened just three years ago," said the child; "that would be since your sister's time."

"Her tragedy?" asked Framton; somehow in this restful country spot tragedies seemed out of place.

"You may wonder why we keep that window wide open on an October afternoon," said the niece, indicating a large French window that opened on to a lawn.

"It is quite warm for the time of the year," said Framton; "but has that window got anything to do with the tragedy?"

"Out through that window, three years ago to a day, her husband and her two young brothers went off for their day's shooting. They never came back. In crossing the moor they were all three engulfed in a piece of bog. Their bodies were never recovered. That was the dreadful part of it."

Here the child's voice lost its self-possessed note and became more human. "Poor aunt always thinks that they will come back someday, they and the little brown spaniel that was lost with them, and walk in at that window just as they used to do. That is why the window is kept open every evening till it is quite dusk."

"Poor dear aunt, she has often told me how they went out, her husband with his white coat over his arm, and Ronnie, her youngest brother, singing 'Bertie, why do you bound?' as he always did. Do you know, sometimes

- **still** = paisible
- **quiet** = calme
- **I almost get a creepy feeling that** = j'ai presque le sentiment terrifiant que
- **to break (broke, broken) off** = s'interrompre
- **a shudder** = un frisson de peur
- **a relief** = un soulagement
- **bustled into the room** = entra dans la pièce d'un air affairé
- **a whirl of apologies** = un tourbillon d'excuses

- **you don't mind** = vous n'êtes pas gêné

- **marshes** = marécages
- **to make a fine mess** = salir
- **So like you menfolk, isn't it ?** = Typiquement masculin, n'est-ce pas ?

- **a less ghastly topic** = un sujet moins épouvantable

- **past him** = par dessus son épaule

- **unfortunate** = malheureuse
- **that he should have paid his visit** = qu'il lui ait rendu visite

- **the doctors agree in ordering me** = tous les médecins sont d'avis de me prescrire
- **rest** = repos
- **on the matter of diet** = en ce qui concerne le régime alimentaire
- **a yawn** = un baillement

on still, quiet evenings like this, I almost get a creepy feeling that they will all walk in through that window—"

She broke off with a little shudder. It was a relief to Framton when the aunt bustled into the room with a whirl of apologies for being late.

"I hope Vera has been amusing you?" she said.

"She has been very interesting," said Framton.

"I hope you don't mind the open window," said Mrs. Sappleton; "my husband and brothers will be home directly from shooting, and they always come in this way. They've been out in the marshes today, so they'll make a fine mess over my poor carpets. So like you menfolk, isn't it?"

She went on gaily about the shooting of birds in the winter. To Framton it was all purely horrible. He made a desperate effort to turn the conversation on to a less ghastly topic, he was conscious that his hostess was giving him only a fragment of her attention, and she was constantly looking past him to the open window.

It was certainly an unfortunate coincidence that he should have paid his visit on this tragic anniversary.

"The doctors agree in ordering me complete rest and an absence of mental excitement," announced Framton. "On the matter of diet they are not so much in agreement," he continued.

"No?" said Mrs. Sappleton repressing a yawn. Then

- **she suddenly brightened** = son visage s'éclaira soudainement

- **Here they are at last!** = Les voilà enfin !
- **muddy up to the eyes** = couverts de boue jusqu'aux yeux

- **to shiver** = frissonner

- **nameless fear** = une peur inommable

- **a figure** = une silhouette

- **noiselessly** = sans aucun bruit
- **to near** = s'approcher
- **hoarse** = rauque

- **to grab** = s'emparer de
- **a stick** = une canne
- **he only dimly noted** = il ne remarqua que vaguement
- **gravel drive** = allée de graviers
- **front gate** = portail
- **hurry** = hâte
- **the hedge** = la haie
- **to avoid** = éviter
- **most extraordinary** = franchement peu ordinaire
- **could only talk** = ne savait parler de rien d'autre
- **an illness** = une maladie
- **to dash off** = se sauver en courant
- **one would think he had seen a ghost** = comme s'il avait vu un fantôme

she suddenly brightened - but not to what Framton was saying.

"Here they are at last!" she cried. "Just in time for tea, and don't they look as if they were muddy up to the eyes!"

Framton shivered and turned towards the niece with a look of sympathetic comprehension. The child was staring out through the open window with horror in her eyes. In a shock of nameless fear Framton turned round and looked in the same direction.

In the deepening twilight three figures were walking across the lawn towards the window, they all carried guns under their arms, and one of them had a white coat over his shoulders. A tired brown spaniel was following them. Noiselessly they neared the house, and then a hoarse young voice chanted: "I said, Bertie, why do you bound?"

Framton grabbed at his stick and hat; he only dimly noted the hall door, the gravel drive, and the front gate in his hurry. A cyclist coming along the road had to run into the hedge to avoid imminent collision.

"Here we are, my dear," said the man with the white coat, coming in through the window. "Who was that who ran out as we came up?"

"A most extraordinary man, a Mr. Nuttel," said Mrs. Sappleton; "could only talk about his illnesses, and dashed off without a word of goodby or apology when you arrived. One would think he had seen a ghost."

- **to expect** = supposer
- **once** = un jour
- **hunted into a cemetery** = poursuivi jusque dans un cimetière
- **the banks** = les rives
- **a pack** = une meute
- **a newly dug grave** = une tombe fraîchement creusée
- **to snarl** = grogner férocement
- **to grin** = montrer les dents
- **foaming** = la gueule écumante
- **Enough to make anyone lose their nerves.** = De quoi avoir les nerfs qui lâchent.
- **a romance** = une fiction / une histoire inventée
- **at short notice** = improvisée

"I expect it was the spaniel," said the niece calmly; "he told me he had a horror of dogs. He was once hunted into a cemetery somewhere on the banks of the Ganges by a pack of dogs, and had to spend the night in a newly dug grave with the creatures snarling and grinning and foaming just above him. Enough to make anyone lose their nerve."

Romance at short notice was her speciality.

~

Achevé d'imprimer en septembre 2016
sur les presses de la **N**ouvelle **I**mprimerie **L**aballery
58500 Clamecy
Dépôt légal : septembre 2016
N° d'impression : 608314

Imprimé en France

La **N**ouvelle **I**mprimerie **L**aballery est titulaire de la marque Imprim'Vert®